This book is the winner of the children's story contest by Inclusive Works, FEBE Support and the British Council Netherlands.

We thank the members of the jury and the chairpersons for their efforts in the contest.

Stereotyping and the depiction of traditional roles for girls and boys starts early in children's lives. This limits their freedom to choose when they are older. Many stereotypes of boys and girls are found in children's books. To break this pattern, we want to expose young children to different roles for boys and girls. That's what this book is for: to make sure that they can make their own choices later on in life.

– FEBE Support

Inclusive Works, in an effort to create a society in which everyone can and wants to participate in an equal way, advises, executes projects, and does research.

– Inclusive Works

Juliëtte S. Rosenkamp & Anouk Nijs

Counting with the Mouse Family

Clavis
NEW YORK

Meet the Mouse family.

They all live together in one house.

Mommy is pretty and loving, and also very strong.
She saws, hammers, and drills at her work.

Daddy does the cooking, ironing, and laundry,
and he watches the little ones.

Little Mouse is the big sister; she's four already.
She loves helping Daddy and Mommy.
And who are the babies of the family?
Take a good look, and see if you can find them.

Daddy Mouse has 1 iron.

He irons a sweater, a skirt, a pair of pants,
a dress, a jacket, and a table cloth.
Little Mouse watches what Daddy does.
Do *you* know how to iron?

2

Mommy Mouse puts 2 garbage bags by the side of the road.

Every week Mommy puts out the garbage for the garbage collectors.
The garbage bags are very heavy.
Do you have muscles like Mommy Mouse?
So big they almost burst out of your sweater?

Daddy Mouse is serving 3 plates of rice and beans.

When Daddy cooks dinner, it's always a feast.
Everyone eats everything on their plates.
Little Mouse wants to know:
What's your favorite food?

S
P

1
2
3
4

Little Mouse has 4 little brothers.

Some of them are hiding!
Looking for them takes Mommy a lot of time.
Can you help? Where are they?
Do you see all of them?

Daddy Mouse is buying 5 things.

He's walking around the supermarket.
Do you see what Daddy is going to buy?
He takes one can of corn
because tonight Daddy is making corn chowder!

2.30
0.99
1.00
2+1
1.20
1.20
1.40
0,80
1.60

Little Mouse has 6 whiskers.

Do you see them?
Three on each side of her snout.
Time to do a little math:
three plus three is… six!

Little Mouse goes to bed at 7.

She brushes her teeth,
washes her hands,
and goes to the potty.
Daddy also puts on
his pajamas. Will you give
the little mice a kiss before they go to bed?

Mommy Mouse takes 8 nails from the toolbox.

She hammers and saws and sands.
Little Mouse helps paint the walls.
Do you know what it sounds like
when Mommy is drilling holes?

Little Mouse has 9 cuddly toys.

Do you see the panda, the pig, and the bear? What other animals do you see? Little Mouse wants to keep them all on her bed. Careful that they don't fall!

Daddy Mouse hangs 10 pairs of underpants on the clothesline.

Do you see the smallest pair?
Can you count all ten?
Here's a difficult question:
How many clothes pins does Daddy use?

First published in Belgium and Holland by Clavis Uitgeverij, Hasselt – Amsterdam, 2013

English translation from the Dutch by Clavis Publishing Inc. New York

Visit us on the web at www.clavisbooks.com

Counting with the Mouse Family written by Juliëtte Rosenkamp
and illustrated by Anouk Nijs
Original title: ***Tellen en rijmen met de familie Muis***
Translated from the Dutch by Clavis Publishing

ISBN 978-1-60537-273-0

This book was printed in January 2016 at Wai Man Book Binding (China) Ltd. Flat A, 9/F., Phase 1,
Kwun Tong Industrial Centre, 472-484 Kwun Tong Road, Kwun Tong, Kowloon, H.K.

First Edition
10 9 8 7 6 5 4 3 2 1

Clavis Publishing supports the First Amendment and celebrates the right to read

CRANBURY PUBLIC LIBRARY
3 9380 00091821 0